GRAFFIX

First paperback edition 1997
Reprinted 1998

First published in hardback by A & C Black (Publishers) Ltd
35 Bedford Row, London WC1R 4JH

ISBN 0-7136-4707-8

A CIP catalogue record for this book is available from
the British Library.

Printed in Great Britain by William Clowes Ltd,
Beccles, Suffolk

Otherworld

Jeremy Strong

Illustrated by Anthony Morris

A & C Black · London

With many thanks to James for all his help.

Chapter One

Alex gazed at the cover of his new VR game. He had picked it up in the market, dirt cheap, from a stall he'd never seen there before. The game was called OTHERWORLD, and it was the picture on the front that had caught his eye.

He turned the box over and read the back, doubting that the game would be anywhere near as good as the extravagant blurb.

OTHERWORLD
Unlike any place on Earth, because it's not on this Earth. Only you can find the beautiful but troubled Tamara, true Princess of Otherworld. But can you save her from the evil sorcerer Grax, and the wicked Queen Morgreth?

OTHERWORLD is a totally new concept in Voice-Activated Virtual Reality games, more like real life than life itself! Play it if you dare!

Alex flipped the disk from its box and switched on the console.

INSERT
OTHERWORLD

As the disc downloaded Alex pulled on his VR helmet and gloves. He glanced at the cover again. There was something about the girl that made him curious. Maybe it was the fear in her eyes and her obvious need for help - his help.

He pulled down his visor. The eye-screen flickered for a moment and then he was flying. Shadowy, dark blue clouds surrounded him. He appeared to be in the high stratosphere above an unknown planet.

Alex was surprised by the brilliant quality of the graphics. The mini-speakers inside his helmet crackled for a moment and then a female electronic voice spoke softly.

Welcome, Alaric.

Alaric? Is that my name?

Affirmative. Approaching Otherworld. Do you wish to land?

'Not yet. Tell me about OTHERWORLD.'

'Atmosphere and appearance similar to Earth, but much smaller in size. The humans are ruled by Queen Morgreth who will stop at nothing to maintain her rule. There are those who say that Tamara, the Wild Princess, is the true ruler of OTHERWORLD, but nobody knows where she is and many have died trying to find her.'

Wicked queens? True rulers?
Talk about predictable!
Uh-oh, here we go...

The craft tilted at a steep angle and the computer-control brought it down on a fast, dipping approach. The voice in Alex's helmet broke in on his thoughts. 'We are being intercepted by a fighter-craft from Morgreth's fleet.' The woman's voice was soft and even, as if she were announcing lunch, and not rapidly approaching death.

Take evasive action.

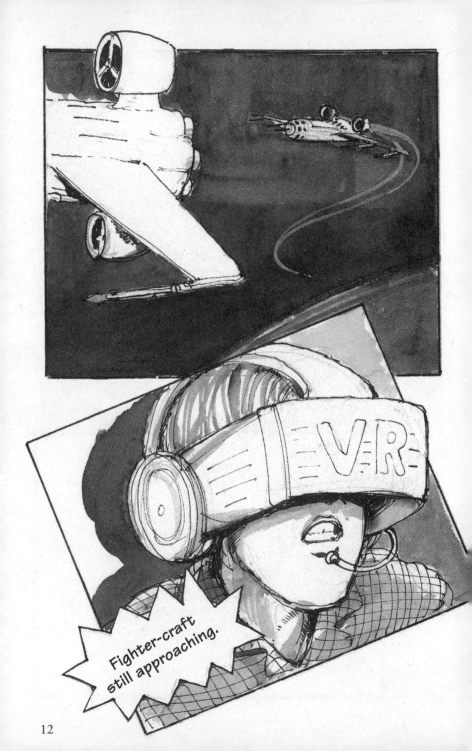

Alex grasped the joystick and pulled it over to the starboard side, plunging after the fighter. But the enemy ship whisked away in a sudden high climb and vanished.

Alex hurled his own ship about, scanning the black sky for the fighter-craft without success. He throttled back, knowing full well that when the enemy disappeared from the screen it would only reappear from another direction with a nice big surprise, such as...

Alex grinned. He didn't think that he was supposed to crash out of the game <u>this</u> early. He thrust the joystick forward and zoomed after the fleeing attacker. Soon he was closing. The enemy craft zig-zagged furiously, but Alex clung on, waiting until his gun-sights were locked on before firing.

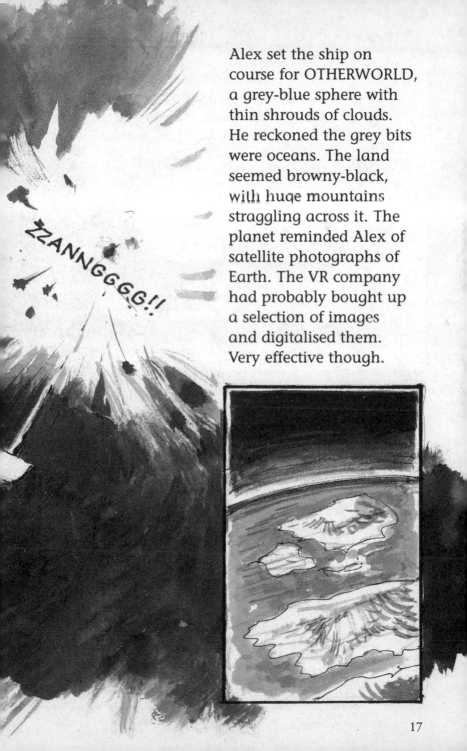

Alex set the ship on course for OTHERWORLD, a grey-blue sphere with thin shrouds of clouds. He reckoned the grey bits were oceans. The land seemed browny-black, with huge mountains straggling across it. The planet reminded Alex of satellite photographs of Earth. The VR company had probably bought up a selection of images and digitalised them. Very effective though.

ZZANNGGGG!!

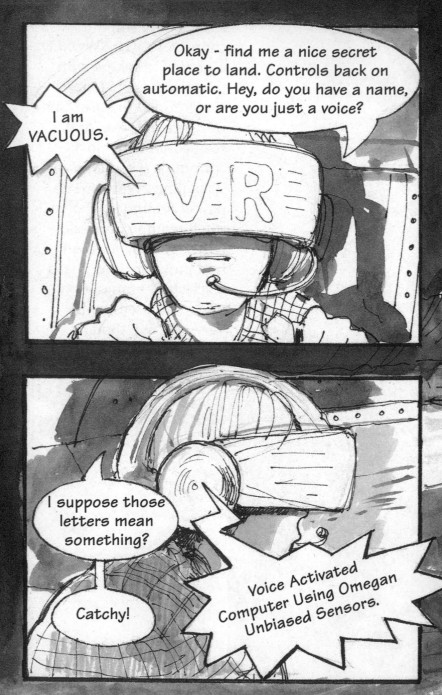

Alex was silent for a moment, watching his instruments as the small ship closed in on OTHERWORLD. Vacuous. Wasn't that a real word? He'd have to look it up.

This looks like a good place to land.

Ahead was the mouth of a large cave and Alex was glad he didn't have to land the craft manually. The Cybership edged forward into the dingy darkness and there was a gentle bump as the ship touched down.

Alex considered his next move. He would have to leave the Cybership, but he had no idea what was out there.

Alaric?

Yes?

Firstly, in order to complete OTHERWORLD you must find Princess Tamara and restore her to the throne.

Secondly, you have only two lives. Please press START to begin, STOP to leave the program, or PAUSE to hold your current position.

Alex pressed PAUSE and pushed up his visor. It was getting dark outside. He idly pushed a pair of jeans across the floor with one foot. The cave on OTHERWORLD had seemed so real. Brilliant graphics! He lifted the VR helmet from his head and laid it carefully on his desk.

From outside came the sound of a heavy truck pulling up. He wandered across to the window and glanced out. The house opposite had been up for sale for months. Now there was a removal truck outside. A battered car pulled into the drive and two people got out.

One was a middle-aged woman, smartly dressed, her face tense. The other was a girl, about his age. She tossed her long, black hair over her shoulders and glanced round the street.

Maybe she saw, or she simply sensed his stare, but she suddenly looked across the road, straight at him. Alex quickly tried to move back out of sight, stumbling over his trainers which were lying on the floor.

That face!
Who is it?
<u>Who</u> is it....????

Thoughts whirled through his mind.

He knew it was someone he had only recently met, and the feeling of knowing and not knowing at one and the same moment was very frustrating.

Chapter Two

Alex was still thinking about the mystery girl at school the following day. He hadn't seen her again, even though he had kept a careful watch from his window almost the whole evening. As he walked down the corridor, he searched his memory for where he might have seen her.

Careful, Alex!

OOOFF!

Sorry...

Oh no, it's her!

Tanya stared directly into Alex's face, making his heart jump. The look was an open challenge and his eyes flinched.

A mischievous spark glinted in Tanya's eyes. Alex was reduced to a stunned, red-faced silence. He wanted to die.

A hush fell the moment Alex led Tanya into the classroom, but it was quickly broken by several wolf-whistles, which did not impress Mr Walker, the Maths teacher. 'Okay boys,' he called. 'This is the age of equality, yes?'

Alex felt oddly protective and he scowled at everyone. All through the lesson he kept glancing across at the new girl, trying to place her. Where did he know her from? Tanya sat there pale and aloof, taking notes. Her long hair fell across her face, but now and then, she tossed back her head, throwing her hair away from her eyes.

Suddenly the revelation of who she was hit Alex like 20,000 volts.

This was the girl on the cover of OTHERWORLD. This was the Wild Princess he was supposed to save. But Tamara was part of a cheap VR game, and Tanya was the real thing. Coincidence?! Alex's brain was rapidly going into overload.

To make matters worse, when the lesson finished things began to get even more complicated - in a way that Alex could well have done without. He had offered to show Tanya round the school, just as he had been asked to do. But as they tried to leave the room Alex was roughly shoved to one side by Biggott, six feet of Neanderthal muscle and no brain.

Biggott was a trouble-maker who liked to throw his weight around, and Alex knew better than to try and argue with him. For the rest of the day Alex couldn't get near Tanya. It was only in their final lesson that he realised that she was not at all happy with her new escort. Tanya had gone up to ask the teacher something, and as she returned to her place she dropped a small piece of crumpled paper on to Alex's desk.

Get me away from that creep or I shall never speak to you again!

As the bell went the whole class rose noisily to their feet. Alex positioned himself between Biggott and Tanya, blocking the doorway. Then he deliberately spilled his bag across the floor, giving Tanya a chance to escape. Biggott tried to push past, but Alex was on his knees, clearing the mess and blocking Biggott's only exit.

A few minutes later Alex found Tanya, standing patiently outside the office. She greeted him with a flashing smile. 'You waited,' he said. 'Thanks.'

'Thanks for getting rid of the gorilla. That guy's a dork. Would you mind walking home with me please. I don't want to end up with him again.'

Alex didn't need to be asked twice, although he secretly wondered what on earth he would do if Biggott turned up. On the way home, Tanya told him a bit about herself.

'My parents split up six months ago - they were always quarrelling, always shouting.'

'Dad was always working late. He'd do anything to keep away from the house. He's a computer expert.'

'Anyway, one afternoon he and Mum had a massive row.'

'Then he just walked out.'

The real problem is my mum. She always wanted to control everything and David, my dad, just got worn out I think.

We've rented the house opposite you. Maybe we'll be able to get on with our lives at last.

Alex didn't know what to say. Tanya was staring straight ahead with fixed eyes. 'That's awful.' Tanya shrugged.

It's not too bad. I've seen Dad since. He's okay, but he won't come back.

They reached the top of their road. Alex was dying to ask Tanya about OTHERWORLD but he wasn't sure what to say.

Tanya glanced across to her own house. Alex could have sworn that she looked scared, and then the moment had passed.

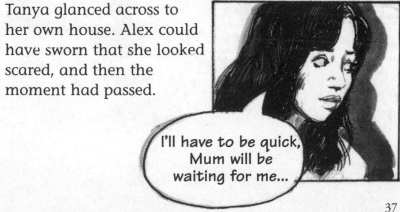

Alex reckoned he'd be a fool to take her to his pig-sty of a room, so he raced upstairs and fetched the VR box, handing it over to Tanya and watching for her reaction. It was not quite what he expected. Certainly she boggled at the picture on the cover.

That's my mum!

But that's you!

This is weird!

They stared at the box. What was going on?

Before they could say another word they were
interrupted by a loud hammering on the front door.
When Alex opened it, he was immediately pushed
aside by Mrs Royce. She stormed into the house,
eyes blazing.

Where's my daughter?
What's going on? Tanya,
come here at once!

Tanya appeared from the front room looking pale,
flustered and just a touch embarrassed.

Mum, it's not what...

Don't say a word!

Mrs Royce seized Tanya
by one arm and
dragged her away.

39

Chapter Three

Alex rushed upstairs, pulled the VR helmet over his head, grabbed the gloves and switched on. If real life was this strange, what was OTHERWORLD going to be like? He had to find Tamara and make sure she really was the same as Tanya.

Alex smiled. Was the computer actually making a joke? Then he began to wonder himself.

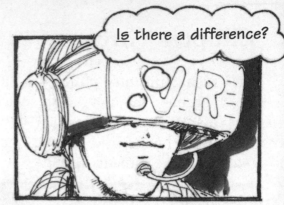

He pushed the start button and found himself looking down a craggy mountainside and across a steep valley to a vast and threatening castle. Once again Alex was impressed by the sheer detail in the program. Its creator must have had to compress several gigabytes to make it this good.

'That must be Castle Catafalque? Do I have any weapons, Vacuous?'
  'You have a sword.'
  'Is that all?'
  'It is the Ancient Sword of Thurgg, Hero of Otherworld.'

Did Thurgg perform mighty deeds with this sword?

He was going to, but the evil sorcerer, Grax, killed him before he could even lift it.

How come?

Sadly Thurgg was a rather small and weak man: too small to lift a big sword.

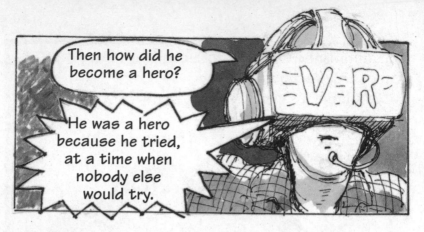

Then how did he become a hero?

He was a hero because he tried, at a time when nobody else would try.

To try when nobody else would try - that appealed to Alex. There were so many things in this game that were different. The cast was the same as most games, and so was the plot, but its creator had put in little unexpected oddities. And then, of course, there were the alarming coincidences.

Alex set off down the mountainside. Condors screeched high above his head, and as he approached the castle the stone monsters on the battlements glared at him sadly.

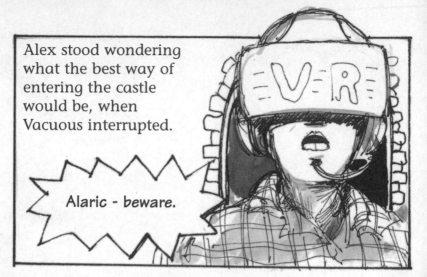

Alex stood wondering what the best way of entering the castle would be, when Vacuous interrupted.

Alaric - beware.

Vacuous was as softly-spoken as usual. Alex put one hand upon his sword hilt ready for action. No sooner had he done so when a huge black snorting horse appeared in front of him, coming from nowhere and everywhere, as pieces of digital information rushed on to the screen from all sides.

WOW!

A disembodied voice rang out, like the echo of a rocket crashing into a ravine.

Alex was so astonished by what he saw, that Grax
had spurred his horse forward before he even had
time to draw his sword. Alex saw the great beast rear
up, its dark shadow blotting out the sunlight.
He heard the hot air snorting from its flared nostrils,
saw Grax's great spear come hurtling at him -
then all went black and quiet.

Alex sank back in his chair. A few moments later the screen cleared and he heard the quiet voice of Vacuous in his ears.

You have lost one of your two lives, Alaric. Do you wish to carry on?

Alex pressed PAUSE, lifted the helmet from his head and wiped the sweat from his frowning brow. First Tanya, then Tanya's mother, and now Biggott. Alex began to wonder if he was going crazy.

Chapter Four

At break the next morning, Alex explained to Tanya what had happened in OTHERWORLD.

It can't have been.

I'll swear it was. Anyway, what was going on yesterday? Why did your mother drag you away like that?

She's very protective. I told you, she likes to control everything. She doesn't like it when I do things for myself. That was one of the things she and Dad used to quarrel about - why he left.

Hmm. Well, she'll have to let go of you sometime.

Oh yeah? She barely lets me out of the house to go to school as it is.

At that moment a dark shadow fell across Alex, and he looked up to find Biggott grinning down at Tanya.

Alex swallowed hard.

She said go away.
She's with me.

Biggott's grin vanished
and was replaced with
an evil leer.

I don't think you
heard me, Whitey.
It's time you went.
Bye bye.

eave him alone,
you thug.

I like a girl with fight in her!

54

A crowd began to gather. Unable to help Alex, Tanya decided to make herself scarce, leaving Biggott scouring the playground for her.

Alex lay crumpled on the floor. He half expected to hear Vacuous break in on his thoughts to tell him he had just lost another life. At least Tanya had managed to escape the gorilla's clutches once again. He sat up, his head aching. He needed a bit of time to think things over. This was getting *TOO WEIRD!*

Alex didn't catch up with Tanya until it was almost lunch-time. The first thing she asked was if he was okay, which Alex found rather pleasing.

I'll live.

Then Alex explained that just as he had lost a life to Grax in OTHERWORLD, he had sort of lost a life to Biggott in this world.

It's like OTHERWORLD is a parallel universe.

Alex felt a strange idea tickling his brain. Maybe the
answer was in OTHERWORLD. If he defeated Grax,
did that also mean he would defeat Biggott?
He couldn't wait to get back home and try again to
rescue the beautiful Tamara.

Chapter Five

Alex's heart was beating very fast as he pulled on the head-set. Within seconds he was out of the real world and back into the dangerous shadows of OTHERWORLD.

With a screech of rusty hinges the huge doors slowly opened. Alex peered into the cobwebbed gloom.

Vacuous?

I am here.

Is Grax in the castle?

Grax is everywhere there is fear. Grax is fear. Fear is Grax. He lives in the darkness of your heart.

Alex wished he hadn't asked.

This sounds like some corny movie!

Alex strode into the Great Hall of the castle, with the Ancient Sword of Thurgg at the ready.

He could hear angry voices in the distance and at once made his way towards them, down a narrow, dark passage. He listened carefully, trying to trace the source of the noise, which gradually became louder. There was a door at the end of the passage. Alex's heart lifted. Surely he had found the princess!

The door was locked.

Alex glanced down at the Sword of Thurgg, thinking that if it was meant to be a key it was rather overdone, but he raised the weapon all the same.

Alex strode into the chamber and with one blow sliced through the ropes that held the princess. She collapsed sobbing into his arms. Queen Morgreth hissed and struck out at him with taloned hands, but he kept her at bay with his sword.

Alex grabbed hold of Tamara's hand and pulled her from the room. Once outside they hurried back along the passage, with Morgreth's mad laughter ringing in his ears.

You might have Tamara, but you'll never escape from Grax and Castle Catafalque! Ha ha ha! Ha ha ha!

As Alex led the princess back to the Great Hall his heart was pounding. There was no doubt, Tamara was the spitting image of Tanya, and although one part of Alex's brain knew that he was in virtual reality he felt as if Tanya was there with him. This was for real - or was it?

As Alex and Tamara entered the Great Hall, they were met by Grax, covered in glistening black armour from head to toe, and holding a double-headed axe. The giant's sneering laugh rang throughout the hollow depths of Castle Catafalque.

Even as Alex watched the sorcerer flap from the screen, he heard a noise behind him.

Swinging round, he came face to face once again with the evil queen.

Alex shook with rage and frustration. Just when he thought he was winning, Tamara had been taken from him. He raised the Ancient Sword of Thurgg high above his head. One blow would get rid of Morgreth for ever, but something made him hesitate.

I will not kill you, old woman. And do not think I will give up now. I will return to rescue Tamara, and if I fail I will return again, and keep on returning, until the rightful Queen of Otherworld is restored to the throne.

Stop, stop! Aaaargh!

The Great Hall fell still and silent. Alex stood alone, panting.

'Vacuous - what's happened?'

'You have destroyed Morgreth.'

Destroyed her? But I didn't touch her!

You killed her with your words.

Alex pressed STOP, and tipped back the VR helmet. How could you kill someone with words? What kind of program-designer would dream up something like this? He had to speak to Tanya.

Alex ran across the road to her house and rang the doorbell. It was not long before Tanya opened it. Her face was very pale and before he could say a word she whispered to him.

So, it's you again! What do you think you're doing here? I've told you to keep away!

Mrs Royce, I've come to talk to Tanya.

No! I forbid it. She talks to nobody!

Mrs Royce lurched forward, her whole face twitching. Alex couldn't help thinking that he was face to face with the Wicked Queen of Otherworld.

Mum!

Mrs Royce, Tanya is thirteen. You can't stop her speaking to people forever.

Alex reached forward and took hold of Tanya's hand. 'Come outside. I want to talk to you.'

Tanya hesitated, looking from Alex to her mother and back again.

'No - nobody can take her from me!' she screeched.

Together they walked quickly down the path, while Mrs Royce stood at the door screaming. But when Alex turned to take another look at her she had vanished, just like the queen. Tanya was shaking. Alex led her across the road to his house.

I've never disobeyed her before.

She'll get over it.

I couldn't have done it without you.

Then he told her about his latest adventures in OTHERWORLD; about how everything that happened there was being repeated in the real world.

Even Morgreth vanished just like your mother. It's spooky.

Maybe. But just remember that Mum hasn't really vanished, and neither has Biggott. Anyway, thanks for what you did. I could never have stood up to her like that.

Will you be all right when you go back?

There's a first time for everything you know!

Tanya gave Alex a strangely beautiful smile that made his face redden, much to his embarrassment.

Chapter Six

Tanya was right. Alex's biggest problem was waiting
for him at school the next day. Alex had arrived at
school with Tanya, and Biggott was already there, his
muscular arms folded across his chest, and a mean
grin plastered across his face.

'I said you were dead meat, Whitey. Keep away
from her - she's mine.'

'Don't be stupid, Biggott. You can't own a person.'

Biggott took a menacing step forward.

But Biggott's mind was single-track and he took another step closer to Alex.

Did you call me stupid?

Alex sighed deeply. All at once he was fed-up with this whole complicated business. He knew he would regret what he said next, but he could no longer help himself.

Yes Biggott, I said you were stupid. That's because you _are_ stupid. You're the stupidest person I've ever...

BAMM

Biggott vanished into the crowd.

'You saved me!' said Alex. 'I thought brave knights were supposed to save princesses, not the other way round!' he joked.